Harvey On Holiday

HARVEY
ON HOLIDAY

TERRANCE DICKS
Illustrated by Susan Hellard

ORCHARD BOOKS
96 Leonard Street, London EC2A 4RH
Orchard Books Australia
14 Mars Road, Lane Cove, NSW 2066
ISBN 1 86039 344 6 (paperback)
First published in Great Britain by Piccadilly Press Ltd
1995
First paperback publication 1997

A CIP catalogue record for this book is available from the British Library.
Printed in Great Britain by
The Guernsey Press Co Ltd, Vale, Guernsey, Channel Islands.

Chapter One

Lost!

"I know where we are," said Mr Smith. "We're lost!"

He jammed his foot on the brake, and the crowded car shuddered to a halt on the dark and misty moor.

"Nonsense!" said his wife in the passenger seat beside him.

"I knew it!" said Harry Smith.

"Oh no!" groaned his sister Sally.

"Woof!" said Harvey, their enormous St Bernard dog.

The two children were crammed into

the back seat of the car. Harvey was stretched out across their feet. Mrs Smith had a folded map on her knee and she was juggling with a compass and one of those map-reading magnifying glasses with a built-in light. Unlike her husband, she was an efficient, well-organised person, and she took getting lost as a personal failure.

"All you have to do is follow my directions," she said. "Carry on down this road, turn off north by north-west and we'll be there in no time."

"I've been following your directions for the last two hours," said Mr Smith wearily. "Look where they've got us. This isn't a road, it's a moorland track – and we're lost!"

"If only you'd listen to what I tell you," said Mrs Smith.

"If only you'd tell me something I could understand," said Mr Smith. "North-west here, south-east there... I'm a simple car driver, not an international airline pilot."

"We're doomed!" said Harry with gloomy relish. "They won't find us for years and years. There'll just be a rusty car full of bleached white skeletons!"

"Shut up you idiot!" said Sally with a shudder.

"WOOF!" said Harvey loudly, and they both shut up.

"What do you think, Harvey?" asked Mr Smith. Harvey tapped the door-handle with a massive paw.

"Harvey wants to get out," said Sally.

"Let him, then," said Harry.

"But he might get lost!"

"We're lost already. Maybe Harvey can find us again."

Harry opened the door and Harvey clambered over their feet and got out. He stood stretching for a moment and then went round to the front of the car, his huge furry shape outlined in the headlights. He looked at Mr Smith, held up one paw for a moment, and then disappeared into the swirling mist.

"I think he wants us to wait," said Mrs Smith.

"Then we'd better wait," said her husband. "Harvey will sort things out."

The Smith family had good reason to trust Harvey. The big St Bernard was a most unusual dog. They'd met him in

Switzerland where they'd gone for a skiing holiday. Harvey was a mountain rescue dog, trained to find and rescue snowbound travellers, a little barrel of brandy around his neck. But progress had made Harvey out of date. These days snowbound travellers carried mobile phones and were rescued by helicopter.

Harvey still wanted to help people but he needed a new job, and he'd decided to look after the Smith family. He had even captured the con-man who'd stolen all their travellers cheques, following them to England in the process.

The grateful Smiths had adopted him, which meant much form-filling and some time in quarantine for Harvey. (Dogs coming into England from abroad have to spend a long time in special kennels, just to make sure they're fit and healthy.) Now, after months of waiting, they were re-united with Harvey and off on holiday again.

Since their holiday in Switzerland had been cut short, the Smiths had decided on a late-summer holiday in Scotland. Unfortunately they'd left it a bit too late, reaching Scotland just as fine summer weather changed to mists and drizzling rain. Now they were lost, somewhere in the heather-covered hills.

"Thank goodness Buster isn't here," said Harry.

Buster was their baby brother, a terrible toddler.

"The trip would have been too much for him," said Mrs Smith.

"It would have been too much for everyone with Buster around!" said Harry.

"I do hope he's happy with Grandma and Grandad."

"Of course he is, Mum," said Sally. "They'll stuff him with sweets, smother him with toys and let him do exactly what he likes."

"That's right," said Harry. "At the moment, good old Buster's a lot better off than we are!"

Huddled together in their car, surrounded by dark shadows and swirling mists, the Smiths waited for Harvey to get them out of trouble again.

Harvey, meanwhile, had reached the top of one of the nearby hills. He stood there for a moment, then slowly revolved in a complete circle. His marvellous St Bernard nose, as efficient as that of any bloodhound, sniffed the night air all around.

Suddenly he froze, pointing. There! The smell of woodsmoke, and of cooking food. Humans!

Harvey turned and bounded back to the car. He stopped in front of it, and gave a loud "Woof!" He trotted on a little way and stopped, looking over his shoulder.

"He wants us to follow him," said Mr Smith in the car.

"Then for goodness' sakes follow, Dad," said Harry. "Harvey knows what he's doing."

Guided by Harvey trotting in front, the car moved slowly over the moor. Stopping occasionally to sniff the misty air, Harvey led them down a narrow winding track and into a little hollow, surrounded by a clump of pine trees. In the middle of the hollow stood a crooked old house, with twisted chimneys and a massive stone doorway. A wooden sign creaked in the night wind.

The Smiths climbed out of the car and stood looking up at the sign.

"The Castle Inn," said Sally.

Harry shuddered. "Looks more like Castle Dracula to me!"

An old fashioned bell-rope hung beside the door. Mr Smith heaved upon it and a bell clanged somewhere inside the house. They heard heavy footsteps clumping towards them. Slowly the massive door swung open. . .

A terrifying figure stood looming in the doorway – a giant of a man in a kilt and a leather jerkin. His huge hairy legs looked like tree-trunks, his brawny arms bulged with muscle and a red beard the size of a doormat spread across his enormous chest.

"Aye?" he growled.

The Smiths were too amazed to speak.

"Weel, what is it ye want?" roared the giant.

"Er – we got lost on the moor," said Mr Smith. "We'd like rooms for the night."

"Season's over – we're no' taking any mair guests," said the giant. He started shutting the door.

He'd reckoned without Mrs Smith. If there was one thing Mrs Smith was keen on it was getting her rights.

"Excuse me," she said sharply. "This *is* an inn, isn't it?"

"Aye, that's what the sign says!"

"Then you have no right to turn us away. An innkeeper is legally obliged to shelter travellers in distress."

Mr Smith wasn't sure if this was true. But the red-bearded giant wasn't sure either. He scratched his head and scowled.

"What's the matter, Angus?"

screeched a high-pitched voice.

A little old lady appeared in the doorway. She had a hooked nose, and long straggly white hair.

"Wow!" whispered Harry. "Not just the gruesome giant but the wicked witch as well!"

His sister Sally jabbed him in the ribs. "Shut up, they're our only hope of a bed for the night."

"There's some Sassenach loons at the door," said the giant. "They claim we're bound to take them in. They say it's the law."

"What did he call us?" asked Harry. "Apart from loons?"

"Sassenachs," said his sister. "It's what the Scots call the English when they don't like them very much."

The old lady came forward, her face twisting in a smile.

"I'd like fine to help you, but the tourist season's over, and the inn's closed for the winter."

"Woof!" The deep, crashing bark made everyone jump. Harvey trotted forward and sat down in front of the little group. He looked solemnly at Angus and the old lady, studying them with his big brown eyes. They looked suddenly uncomfortable.

"Still, we canna turn ye away," said the old lady, almost in spite of herself. "Not on a night like this."

"But mam," protested the giant.

The old lady jumped up and boxed his ears. "Shut up, Angus, ye great gowk! Would you have them go about the countryside complaining about us? Fetch their luggage!" She beckoned to the Smiths. "In ye come then, since you must. We're simple folk but I'm sure we can take care of you."

They all followed her into the house. Angus came behind with the luggage, and the great door slammed shut behind them.

Chapter Two
The Sinister Inn

Harry finished his second plate of stew. "Delicious!"

The old lady – her name was Mrs Macavity – said, "Simple fare, but it's the best we can manage."

They were eating in the big kitchen. A fire blazed in the open grate. Harvey was stretched out in front of it. Like the Smiths, he was full of stew.

There was only one other guest, a tall, dark and handsome but stern-faced man who sat at the other end of the long wooden table. The old lady introduced him as Mr Jones.

"Another late traveller, like yourselves. He turned up last night, and persuaded us to take him in."

Mr Jones nodded grimly, and got on with his meal. He seemed worried and obviously didn't want to talk.

When the meal was over he stood up, muttered, "Goodnight," and made for the door.

As he passed by Harvey he paused. "You're a fine big fellow, aren't you?" He looked at the Smiths. "What's his name?"

"Harvey," said Sally.

Mr Jones stroked Harvey's head, Harvey thumped his tail on the floor, and Mr Jones went out of the kitchen.

"Well, he must be all right if Harvey likes him," said Harry.

"More than he does the Macavitys," whispered Sally. "When they stroked him he just ignored them."

Mrs Macavity said, "I expect you'll be wanting your beds. You'll be making an early start for the Games, the morn's morn."

"Games?" said Mr Smith.

"The Highland Games," said Mrs Macavity. She stared suspiciously at them. "That is why you're here, isn't it?"

"Yes, of course," said Mrs Smith, always a keen tourist. "The Highland Games. We wouldn't miss them."

Angus led them up a stone staircase and turned right, along a gloomy corridor. They caught a glimpse of Mr Jones going into a room at the far end.

Angus pointed to a door. "There's a fine big bedroom just there, with two smaller ones next to it. I take it the dog will go in with one of you? Or will he be needing his own room?"

Harvey sat down in the corridor.

"Looks as if he's staying right here," said Harry.

"He can please himself," said Angus. He stomped away.

All three rooms were much the same – gloomy and old-fashioned with big beds and heavy furniture.

Mrs Smith sniffed. "The whole place is damp and musty – you'd think it hadn't been used for ages."

"I expect we'll survive till morning," said Mr Smith.

"If the ghosties and ghoulies don't get us," said Harry.

"What are you on about?" asked Sally uneasily.

"It's a poem." In a spooky voice, Harry recited:

"From ghosties and ghoulies
And long-legged beasties
And things that go bump in the night
May the Good Lord deliver us!"

"Thanks a lot," said Sally. "That's really cheered me up!"

Their parents said goodnight, and went off to their room.

Sally and Harry both tried to persuade Harvey to join them.

"Come on Harvey," coaxed Sally. "You can sleep on the bed, if you promise not to push me out."

Harvey refused to budge.

"Leave him alone," said Harry. "I think he wants to stay out here on guard." They went off to bed.

Harvey lay stretched out in the corridor. As Harry said, he was on guard. Dogs are very sensitive to atmosphere, and Harvey felt there was something very strange about this place. Something dangerous.

After a while he heard low voices from downstairs. Harvey got to his feet and padded silently along the corridor. He reached the head of the stairs and looked down.

The Macavitys were sitting at the kitchen table.

"You should not have taken these people in," Angus was saying. "It was a mistake – just as with the man Jones, last night."

"It was necessary," snapped Mrs Macavity. "This is supposed to be an inn. We cannot afford to rouse suspicion. Suppose we turned them away and they complained to the police? Besides, it is only for one more night. Tomorrow we carry out The Plan. After that we shall both be gone."

Their voices were harsh and clear, with no trace of the broad Scottish accents they'd used earlier.

"It would be safer to dispose of them all," said Angus.

"Certainly not! There must be no trouble, nothing unusual. Tomorrow they will go and – "

Suddenly she broke off. "Listen!"

"What is it?"

Mrs Macavity looked up at the ceiling. "Footsteps! There's someone in the office!"

Angus leapt from his chair and ran up the stairs.

Harvey moved back into the corridor as Angus reached the head of the stairs. Angus turned left into the other corridor, with Harvey padding behind him.

Angus threw open a door and Harvey caught a brief glimpse of a dark shape crouching by a desk. With a bellow of rage, Angus rushed into the room, slamming the door behind him.

From behind the door came the sounds of a tremendous struggle. There were shouts and yells and bangs and thumps. . .

With the door shut, there was nothing Harvey could do. He let out a series of his loudest barks to raise the alarm. "Woof! Woof! WOOF!"

Mrs Macavity came panting along the corridor followed by the Smith family in their night clothes.

"What's happening, Harvey?" shouted Harry.

"My son Angus has caught a burglar," said Mrs Macavity.

Suddenly Harvey realised that the sounds of struggle had stopped. He looked at the door and gave another urgent, "Woof!"

"We'd better see what's going on," said Mr Smith.

"No, no," said Mrs Macavity hurriedly, "Angus will deal with him."

"He may need help," said Mr Smith bravely, and opened the office door.

The room was empty!

Harvey looked inside. He saw an overturned desk and a broken chair, with a litter of papers on the floor. The bedroom window was open.

"Looks as if he got away out of the window," said Mrs Smith.

"My Angus must have chased after him," said Mrs Macavity.

"We'd better call the police," said Mrs Smith.

Mrs Macavity shook her head. “No need for that.”

“But surely – ”

“We canna call the police, the phone’s no’ working.”

Suddenly they heard the big front door open and close. They all hurried downstairs, and saw Angus in the hall.

“It was a burglar richt enough,” he said. “I chased him out the windae, but he got clean away.” He took a shotgun down from the wall. “I’ll be staying on guard the rest o’ the nicht. You’ll do well to go back to your rooms and stay there. We dinna want any accidents.”

The Smiths beat a hasty retreat. Mr and Mrs Smith went back to bed, but Harry and Sally paused in the corridor to talk.

“There’s something funny about all this,” said Harry. “What about Mr Jones? What happened to him?”

“Maybe he slept through it all,” said Sally.

“Let’s go and see,” said Harry. “His room’s along here.”

They went along to the room and Harry tapped on the door. There was no reply. Harry tried the door – it was open. They looked inside. The room was empty, and the bed was still made up. There was a half-unpacked suitcase on the floor.

“Weird!” said Harry. “Where’s he got to? And come to that, where’s Harvey?”

Harvey was in the burgled office, looking around curiously. He went over to the still-open window and looked out. It wasn’t much of a drop. Harvey bounded through the window and landed on the ground below. He started sniffing around, picked up the trail and followed it into the darkness.

The trail didn’t lead him very far – just to a garden hut on the edge of the inn grounds. Harvey sniffed at the door and stood up on his hind legs, hitting the door with his big front paws.

The door swung open, revealing a dark shape on the ground. It was a man, and he was bound and gagged. He was wriggling furiously, trying desperately to get free.

"Woof!" said Harvey softly. He lowered his head and began gnawing at the ropes that bound the man's wrists.

Chapter Three
DANGER IN THE MOUNTAINS

The Smiths were up and ready to go first thing. The mist had cleared, it was a fine sunny morning and they were eager to be on their way. Mrs Macavity served them a breakfast of porridge and oatcakes.

Harvey had porridge as well. He sniffed it a bit suspiciously, at first, tried it, and lapped up a big bowl.

"What happened to Mr Jones?" asked Harry.

"Oh, he had to leave at crack of

dawn," said Mrs Macavity. "He had a very early appointment somewhere far away."

Harry looked at Sally, but he didn't say anything. When they went up to get their things they had a quick look in Mr Jones's room. The bed had been stripped and the suitcase was gone.

"Don't say anything about it," said Sally. "Let's just get out of here!"

When they came downstairs their parents were in the hall, trying to pay the bill. Mrs Macavity wouldn't hear of it.

"I canna charge you a penny," she said firmly. "You were poorly looked after, and ye had a disturbed night as well. If I dinna charge you, you canna complain!"

The Smiths tried to insist but it was no use. They piled into the car, waved goodbye to the Macavitys and set off.

Mr Smith was puzzled but pleased as they drove away across the moor. "I thought that was very generous, not charging us. So much for those silly stories about Scottish people being mean!"

"They were very keen that we shouldn't complain about them," said Mrs Smith. "Almost as though they'd got something to hide."

"I think they had," said Harry. He told them about the mysterious disappearance of Mr Jones.

"There was something else strange about them," said Sally. "They were just *too* Scottish. As if they were playing a part."

Mrs Smith had her map out and was studying it. "Now, if we head north, north-east. . ."

"Here we go again!" groaned Mr Smith.

Harvey sat up, leaned over the front seat, and plonked a massive paw down on the map.

"Look," said Mrs Smith. "He's pointing

to the castle where they're holding the Highland Games."

Mr Smith stopped the car. "All right, Highland Games here we come. But this time you drive and I'll navigate!" Snatching up the map, he got out of the car and waved his wife towards the driving seat.

Mrs Smith got behind the wheel and Mr Smith sat beside her, studying the map. "It's quite simple. To reach the Highland Games we have to get past these mountains." He pointed. "We'll save hours of driving if we cut through this mountain pass – here!"

Mrs Smith looked at the map. "Wouldn't it be safer to go round? That pass looks pretty steep. Suppose it's snowed in?"

"Not at this time of year," said Mr Smith confidently. "I'm navigating, and I say we go this way."

"All right, all right," said Mrs Smith. She started the car.

Soon after the Smiths drove away across the moor, Mrs Macavity was closing the front door of the inn. Suddenly Angus appeared. "The spy Jones has escaped. His ropes have been *chewed!*"

"That dog!" said Mrs Macavity. "I knew he suspected us. No matter. We can still carry out The Plan. And if Jones or the dog get in our way. . ."

"If they do, I shall deal with them," snarled Angus.

They jumped into their waiting Land Rover and drove away.

It was sheer bad luck that the mist came down again. It was several hours later and the Smiths' car was on a narrow mountain road, climbing all the time. The higher they climbed, the mistier it got and the more anxious the Smiths became.

"Turn the radio on, Mum," said Harry. "Maybe some music will cheer us up."

Mrs Smith turned on the radio and they got a burst of pop music mixed up with crackles. She was just about to turn it off again when there was a sudden newsflash. "*An extraordinary and shocking crime took place in Scotland just a short time ago,*" said the excited announcer. "*By using forged papers, identifying himself as a veterinary surgeon, a man obtained entrance to the kennels at Balmoral. He overpowered two security guards, and kidnapped the royal corgis. Police and army are currently searching for the man, who is described as being large and muscular, with a red beard. . .*"

Harry nudged Sally. "You know who that sounds like. . ."

The newsflash faded out in a crackle of static and Mrs Smith turned off the radio. Suddenly a shape loomed up out of the mist and she jammed on the brakes.

The shape turned out to be a big Land Rover parked by the side of the road, with two men standing beside it. One of them, a thick-set man in an anorak came up to the car. He had a knapsack on his shoulder. Mrs Smith

wound down the window.

"What the blazes are you doing here?" asked the man.

"We're lost," said Mrs Smith. "What's your excuse?"

"We're part of a mountain rescue team. We're looking for a man stranded on the mountain side. We think he's had some kind of accident. He seems to be hurt. A helicopter spotted him close

to a wrecked car a while back, but the mist came down and they lost him. We're sure he's somewhere near, but we canna find him."

"Woof!" said Harvey. "Woof! Woof! Woof!"

"What's the matter with your dog?" asked the man.

"Harvey wants to help," said Sally.

"He's a trained mountain rescue dog,"

said Harry. "It was his full-time job back in Switzerland."

The man looked at Mr and Mrs Smith. "Could you lend us the dog for a wee while? It's our last chance. If we dinna find him soon the poor fellow's done for."

"Of course we will," said Mr Smith. Sally opened the door and got out. "Come on, Harvey!"

Harvey jumped out after her and Harry jumped out as well.

"We'll go and help," he said. "See you back here."

Before Mr and Mrs Smith could object, they all disappeared into the mist.

Happy to be doing the job he was born for, Harvey bounded up the mountain side. He wished he had his little barrel of brandy around his neck, but you can't have everything.

Harry and Sally, and the mountain rescue man, whose name was Hamish, followed after him. The other man, who was called Mac, was manning the radio in their Land Rover.

Every now and then Harvey paused to sniff the wind. He led them higher and higher until they were scrambling amidst rocky gullies filled with snow.

"Too early for snow really," said Hamish. "Must have been a freak storm. I'm afraid we may be too late."

Suddenly Harvey stopped and sniffed again. He dashed over to one gully and started digging. Snow flew from between his giant paws and in no time at all a foot appeared. The others ran to help and uncovered a huddled and shivering shape.

For a moment Sally was afraid that they really were too late, and then the man shuddered and opened his eyes.

"Good old Harvey," he said weakly. "You've saved me again!"

It was Mr Jones – the man who'd vanished from the inn.

Chapter Four
Harvey's Reward

"The Castle Inn closed down weeks ago," said Mr Jones. "The Macavitys moved in and pretended to be the new owners. I suspected they were up to no good. That's why I was staying at the inn – to check up on them."

"Look, who are you, really?" said Harry.

"The name's B... On second thoughts, perhaps you'd better just go on calling me Jones. James Jones. My job's security. When the Royals are in residence we keep an eye on the whole countryside. Anyway, I was searching Mrs Macavity's office to find out what they were up to when that big brute Angus came up behind me. He knocked me out and tied me up in a shed. Luckily, Harvey here came to my rescue." He stroked Harvey's head. "Then he turned up here and rescued me all over again."

"That's what Harvey does," said Harry. "He's a rescue dog!"

Harvey, who had been listening keenly, gave a modest "Woof!"

"How did you end up here on the mountain?" asked Sally.

"After Harvey turned me loose, I waited in my car and tailed the Macavitys. They must have realised I was following them. Angus waited in ambush and blasted my tyres with his shotgun. My car went over the edge of the road, I jumped out, and ended up in this gully with a sprained ankle. I think a helicopter spotted me, but then the mist came down."

They were sheltering in the little gully under a metallic silver space blanket provided by Hamish, who had gone off to send for help with the radio in his Land Rover. He'd strapped up Mr Jones's ankle and he'd left them a flask of hot coffee and some emergency rations, which they'd scoffed up eagerly.

"What worries me is, I still haven't found out what the Macavitys are up to," said Mr Jones, swigging his coffee.

"I think we can tell you that," said Sally. She told him the news about the kidnapped corgis.

"So *that's* who they are. . . " Mr Jones looked thoughtful.

"Perhaps they've got a secret hideout up here?" suggested Harry.

"If they have, it won't be far away," said Mr Jones.

He clambered to his feet. "Harvey, you know the Macavity scent. You've got to find them for me, before they move on!"

"Woof!" said Harvey. He stretched his nose up into the air and sniffed the breeze. Then he set off along the rocky path. Mr Jones hobbled after him, supported by Harry and Sally.

Harvey led them higher still, to a ruined hut at the top of the mountain pass. They studied it from behind some rocks.

"Looks like an old climbing shelter," said Mr Jones. "Seems to be empty. Let's wait a bit."

After what seemed like ages there was a noise and they saw a Land Rover appearing from the other side of the pass. A white-haired figure appeared in the doorway of the shelter. It was Mrs Macavity. The Land Rover drew up before the little house and Angus got out. He opened the back door of the Land Rover, and reached inside. Five little brown dogs jumped out, on the end of a five-dog leash. Angus led them inside the hut and Mrs Macavity followed.

"The royal corgis!" whispered Mr Jones."We've found them!"

"Hang on," said Harry. "You're in no shape for any heroics."

"It's my duty," said Mr Jones. "Don't worry, I can handle the Macavitys."

Drawing an automatic, he hobbled up

to the door of the hut. Harry and Sally and Harvey followed close behind. Mr Jones threw open the door. “Hands up – you’re under arrest!”

Mrs Macavity was herding the yapping corgis into a travelling-cage in the corner of the hut. She whirled round.

Mr Jones looked round the hut. “Where’s Angus?”

Harry saw an open door on the other side of the hut.

“Look out,” he shouted – but it was too late.

“I’m right here, Mr Jones,” said a familiar voice. Angus had circled the hut and got behind them. Now he was covering them with his shotgun. “Inside,” he barked. “Jones, drop that gun.”

Mr Jones obeyed. They moved inside the hut – all except Harvey. Suddenly he turned and lolloped away. Angus raised his gun.

"No!" yelled Sally and pushed the gun in the air. It exploded harmlessly and Harvey disappeared into the mist.

Mrs Macavity snatched up Mr Jones's automatic. "Never mind the dog – cowardly great beast! It can't give evidence against us."

Angus reloaded his shotgun. "Nor will these three when I'm done with them. A nice little car crash, I think."

Mr Jones said grimly, "You won't get away with this!"

"No?" sneered Angus. "As soon as this mist clears, our friends will come in a helicopter and whisk us away from here to a safe hideout."

Angus backed towards the door, waving the shotgun. "Outside, all of you. Time you had your accident!"

Mrs Macavity raised the automatic.

"Move!"

Harry and Sally and Mr Jones looked helplessly at each other. They were covered from both sides – the situation was hopeless.

Something thumped the hut door hard and it burst open, sending Angus staggering back. Harvey bounded into the hut and leaped straight at Angus, knocking him clean off his feet. Mr Jones threw himself at Mrs Macavity, wrenching the automatic from her hand.

Suddenly the hut was full of burly figures in anoraks – Hamish and the rest of his mountain rescue team.

Holding Angus down with his paws, Harvey tugged his red beard with his mouth. Hair and beard came away in one piece, revealing a beardless man with a jutting jaw and a bald head.

Mr Jones snatched off Mrs Macavity's white wig, and her false nose, showing her to be a much younger woman.

"Just as I thought," said Mr Jones. "A well-known pair of international criminals. They kidnap the pets of millionaires all over the world. It's a very clever ploy – wealthy people are used to protecting themselves and their families from kidnappers but not their pets. These two have managed to swindle people of loads of money – most of them really care about their pets and are prepared to pay the ransoms for their safe return."

He looked at Hamish and the others. "How did you lot manage to find us in time?"

"When we got to the gully where I'd left you, Harvey was waiting," explained Hamish. "He brought us here. Mac sent your message for you – the Army are on their way."

"We'd better tie these two up," said

Mr Jones. "Anyone got any rope?"

One of the mountain rescue team produced a coil of rope.

Sally turned to Hamish, "Do you think you could guide us back to our car – and then direct us to to the nearest hotel? I think Mum and Dad have had enough excitement for one night."

"My sister runs a little hotel near here," said Hamish. "I'd be happy to take you there myself."

"Come on Harvey," said Harry. They slipped away into the mist.

"Well, this is certainly something," said Mr Smith. "Harvey, you made the right decision!"

"Woof!" said Harvey.

It was the next day and the sun was shining again. After a night in a nice, and definitely non-sinister hotel, they'd reached the Highland Games at last.

Beneath the shadow of the gloomy old castle, the Games formed a lively, busy scene. The Smiths walked through the cheerful crowd, looking all around them. There were brawny Scotsmen throwing the hammer or tossing the caber – a caber seemed to be a kind of tree-trunk.

There was Highland dancing and the swirl of bagpipes.

There were stalls selling Highland crafts and produce, everything from Scotch whisky to smoked salmon. Harvey studied it all with solemn interest. He'd seen nothing like it in Switzerland. The bagpipes upset him a bit. Dogs have very keen hearing. Harvey lifted his head and howled when the bagpipes played, and the Smiths had to drag him away.

They were watching the finals of the hammer-throwing championships when someone called, “Hey, you lot – I’ve been looking everywhere for you!”

They turned and saw Mr Jones running towards them.

“What do you mean by sneaking off last night?” he demanded.

“Are we in trouble?” asked Harry.

“Just the opposite!” said Mr Jones. “A certain Very Important Person is just going to present the prize cup for the hammer throwing – but she wants to thank your furry friend here first. Come on Harvey!”

Obediently, Harvey trotted off after him.

They watched as Mr Jones took Harvey up on to the platform where the Very Important Person had just arrived. This particular VIP turned out to be a surprisingly small lady in a raincoat and headscarf, surrounded by a bodyguard of Army officers. One of them was holding five little corgis on a combined leash.

Mrs Smith looked at the Queen and gasped, "But surely that's – "

"Yes it is, Mum," said Sally. They all watched as Mr Jones led Harvey up to the Queen. She bent down and chatted to him for a moment, and held out her hand. Bowing his head, Harvey offered her his paw and they shook hands.

One of the Army officers handed the Queen his sword.

Harvey sat down and she tapped him with the sword, first on one shoulder and then on the other. Then she hung a shining gold medal on a blue satin ribbon around his neck. Everyone cheered. The Queen patted Harvey on the head and moved away.

Harvey trotted proudly back towards the Smiths, the gleaming medal around his neck.

"What on earth is going on?" demanded Mrs Smith.

"Has Harvey won some kind of prize?" asked Mr Smith.

"You might say that," said Sally.

"Not so much of the plain 'Harvey', Dad," said Harry. "You'll have to call him Sir Harvey from now on!"